# HAYYIM'S GHOST

RETOLD BY
# ERIC A. KIMMEL

ILLUSTRATED BY **ARI BINUS**

PITSPOPANY

NEW YORK ◇ JERUSALEM

**Author's Note:**
This story is based on "The Tale of A Stingy Woman" in Beatrice Silverman Weinreich's *Yiddish Folktales* (Pantheon, 1988). It was originally told by Shoshe Halkon and recorded in Grodno in 1928.

HAYYIM'S GHOST

Published by Pitspopany Press
Text Copyright © 2004 by Eric A. Kimmel
Illustrations Copyright © 2004 by Ari Binus

Design: Benjie Herskowitz

Hard Cover ISBN: 1-932687-02-5
Soft Cover ISBN: 1-932687-03-3

Pitspopany Press titles may be purchased for fund raising programs
by schools and organizations by contacting:

Marketing Director, Pitspopany Press
40 East 78th Street, Suite 16D
New York, New York 10021
Tel: (800) 232-2931
Fax: (212) 472-6253
Email: pitspop@netvision.net.il
Website: www.pitspopany.com

Printed in Israel

In loving memory of Ethan S. Naftalin z"l

Ari Binus

# Also by ERIC A. KIMMEL

## THE BRASS SERPENT

What is the Biblical origin of the symbol of the doctor's healing power, a staff with a snake curled around it?

*Winner of*
**The 2004 World Storytelling Award**

## Why The Snake Crawls On Its Belly

Why did the snake lose it's legs?
Why does it shed it's skin?
Why does it have a forked tongue?

*National Jewish Book Award Finalist*

# HAYYIM'S GHOST

# Many years ago

an inn stood on the road to Horodenka. Reb Aaron, the innkeeper, was a little man with a red beard. That is all anyone remembers about him.

His wife, Bayla Esther, was another story. Everyone remembers her only too well.

Bayla Esther was twice as tall as her husband, strong as a bear and fierce as a Cossack. She fought with everyone, even the rabbi. She could not speak without cursing. It was said that she even swore in her sleep.

Bad enough that Bayla Esther was a shrew; she was also a miser. She never gave a penny to charity, and every beggar in town knew better than to ask for alms at the inn. She even begrudged Reb Aaron the thin soup and dry bread he ate. Heaven help the poor man if he asked for more!

So it came as no surprise when Bayla Esther awoke one morning to find her husband dead. Did she weep? Did she mourn?

Not one bit! The first thought to come into Bayla Esther's mind was, "That worthless man! Now I will have to pay money to bury him!" Not that she would have to pay that much. The Hevra Kadishah – the Burial Society – arranged all funerals in Horodenka. They made no distinction between rich or poor. Everyone was buried the same way, with honor and dignity. Everyone in Horodenka, even a homeless wanderer, was assured a dignified funeral and a final resting place.

Bayla Esther didn't care about honor or dignity. She didn't care if her husband received a decent burial or not. All that worried her was having to pay for it. Rich as she was, the Burial Society would expect a large donation in Reb Aaron's name. But what if no one knew they were burying Reb Aaron?

Bayla Esther's fingers twitched as she thought out her plan. She tore up some old bedsheets and sewed them together to make burial clothes for her husband. After dressing him, she covered his face and wrapped his body in another large sheet. Then she went to the market.

Here she found Hayyim the porter. Hayyim was also a little man with a red beard, who looked enough like Reb Aaron to be his brother. He earned his living carrying bundles and helping people move furniture.

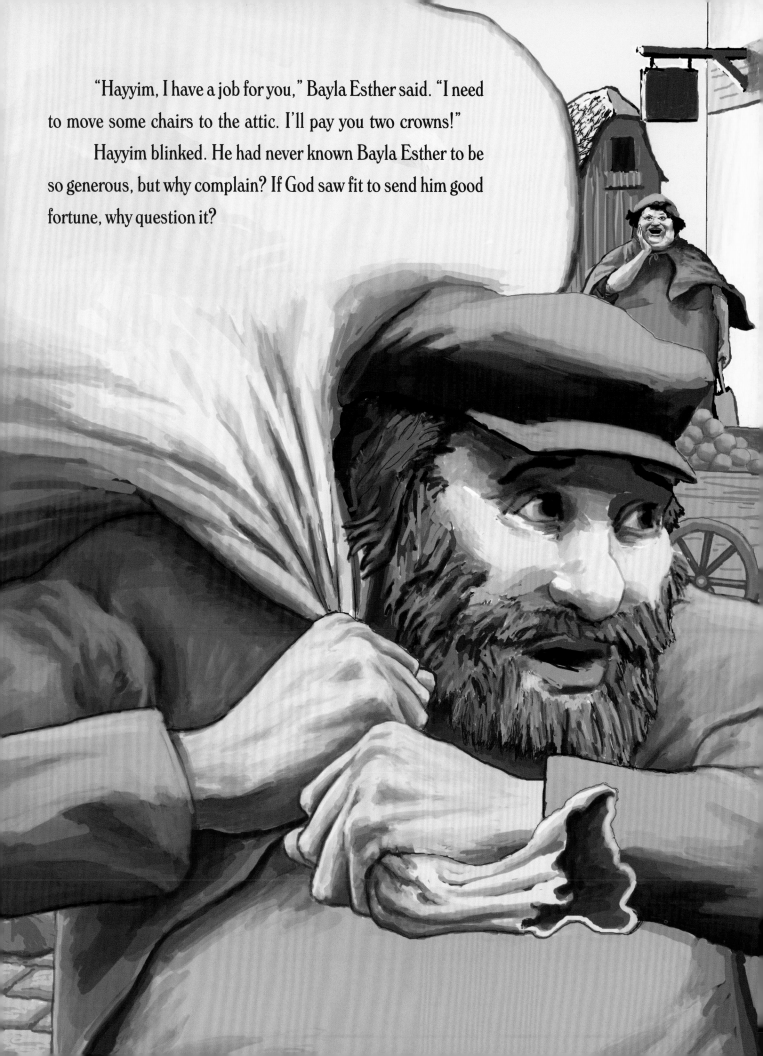

"Hayyim, I have a job for you," Bayla Esther said. "I need to move some chairs to the attic. I'll pay you two crowns!"

Hayyim blinked. He had never known Bayla Esther to be so generous, but why complain? If God saw fit to send him good fortune, why question it?

Hayyim followed Bayla Esther to the inn. He carried four chairs up to the attic. Bayla Esther paid him two gold crowns. Hayyim was overjoyed. Then Bayla Esther said to him, "You've worked well, Hayyim. You deserve a drink."

She filled a big glass with plum brandy.
"That's an awful lot of brandy," Hayyim said.
"What do you care?" Bayla Esther replied. "Drink it down!"
Hayyim raised the glass and made a toast: "L'hayyim!"

He giggled
at his little joke.
L'hayyim means
"To life!"
It also means,
"To Hayyim!"
Bayla Esther
didn't laugh.
"Have another."
She filled up the
glass again.
Hayyim drank
it down.

"And another."

Hayyim's head began to spin. "I've had enough, Bayla Esther. This brandy is very strong."

"Drink!"

Hayyim downed the third glass.
He staggered across the room.
"Bayla Esther, help me!
I need to lie down."

"There's an empty room upstairs. You
can stay there until you feel better." Bayla
Esther half-lifted, half-carried Hayyim up
the stairs. By the time she got him to the bed,
he was unconscious.

"Sleep well.

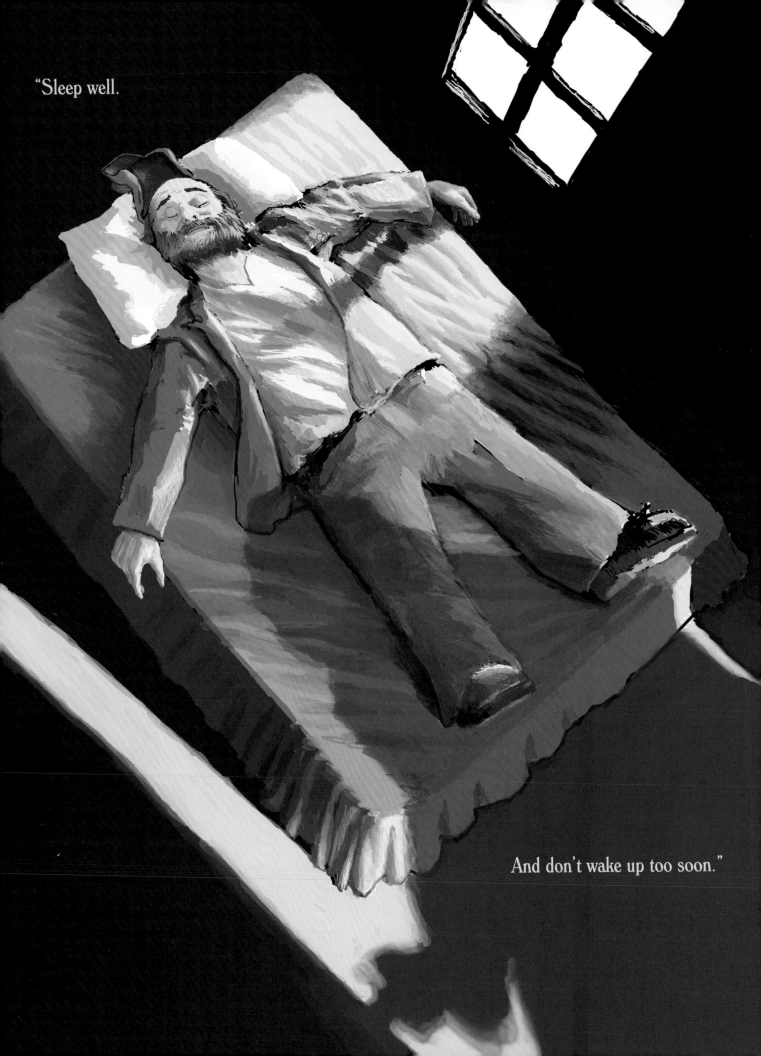

And don't wake up too soon."

Bayla Esther took Hayyim's clothes. She carried them to her own room, where poor Reb Aaron lay dead. Bayla Esther dressed her husband in Hayyim's clothes. She didn't forget to remove the two gold crowns from his pocket. Then she carried Reb Aaron's shroud and grave clothes back to the other room, where she dressed Hayyim like a corpse ready for burial.

Bayla Esther sent for the rabbi. "Poor Hayyim! He was helping me move chairs. Suddenly he fell down dead!"

The rabbi saw a little man dressed as a porter lying on the bed. A handkerchief covered his face; the tip of a red beard peeking out from underneath the hem.

"I will tell Hayyim's wife, poor woman," the rabbi said. "We must summon the Hevra Kadishah."

The Burial Society came within the hour. They prepared the body, placed it in a coffin, and carried it to Hayyim's house for the funeral. No one looked too closely to see if the dead man really was Hayyim the porter, which was just what Bayla Esther had hoped for.

Everyone in Horodenka came to the cemetery.
Hayyim was a poor man, so his family was not expected
to pay for his funeral – which meant that Bayla Esther
succeeded in burying her husband for free!
What about the real Hayyim?

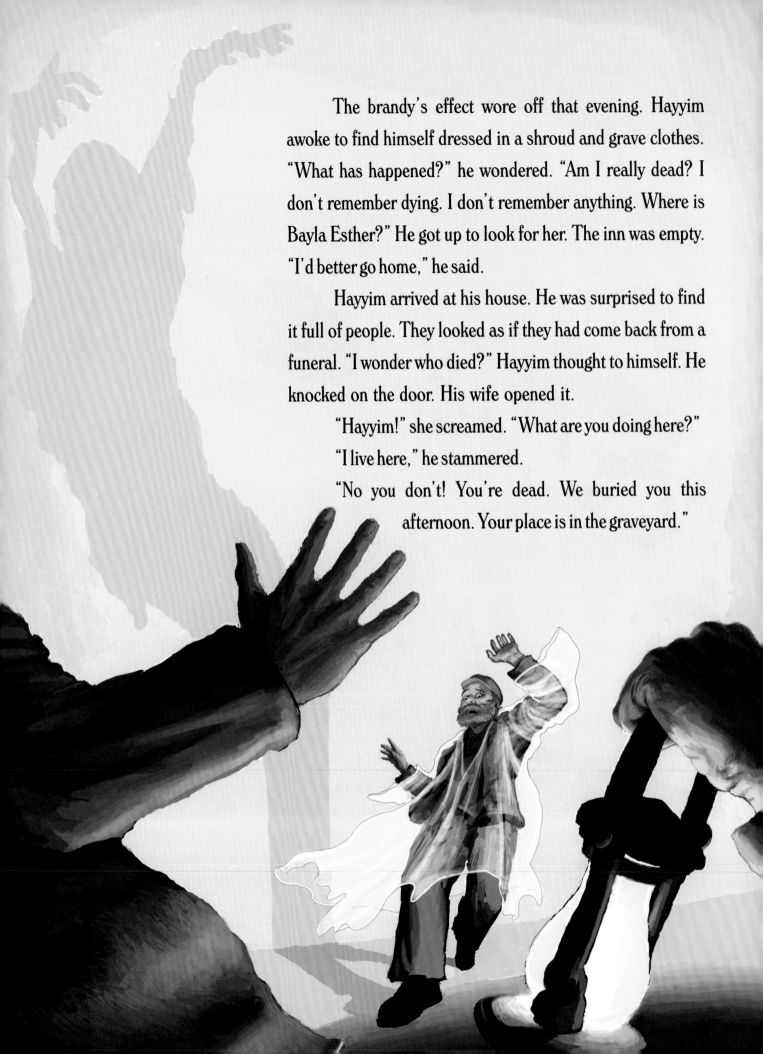

The brandy's effect wore off that evening. Hayyim awoke to find himself dressed in a shroud and grave clothes. "What has happened?" he wondered. "Am I really dead? I don't remember dying. I don't remember anything. Where is Bayla Esther?" He got up to look for her. The inn was empty. "I'd better go home," he said.

Hayyim arrived at his house. He was surprised to find it full of people. They looked as if they had come back from a funeral. "I wonder who died?" Hayyim thought to himself. He knocked on the door. His wife opened it.

"Hayyim!" she screamed. "What are you doing here?"

"I live here," he stammered.

"No you don't! You're dead. We buried you this afternoon. Your place is in the graveyard."

"Go back, spirit! You don't belong among the living!" the other mourners cried.

"Is this true?" Hayyim asked himself. "I'd better talk to the rabbi. He will know what has happened to me."

Hayyim hurried to the rabbi's house. Everyone he met along the street ran away, as if they had seen a ghost. He knocked at the rabbi's door.

"Hayyim, what are you doing here?" the rabbi said, his face turning pale with fright.

"I came to ask you a question, Rabbi. Am I alive, or dead?"

"Of course you're dead! We buried you this afternoon. I myself led the service. I understand that you feel lonely and frightened, Hayyim, but your place is no longer among the living. You must go back to the graveyard. I will pray that your soul may find peace. You must not come here again!"

Hayyim turned away. "If the rabbi says I am dead, then it must be true." He walked back to the cemetery. There he sat on the wall, thinking about life and death. He sat there all night.

In the morning he saw his friend Mottel the baker coming up the road to market. He carried a basket of loaves, fresh from the oven.

"Hello, Mottel!" Hayyim called, forgetting that he was supposed to be dead. Mottel screamed. He threw down the basket and ran off. Hayyim picked up the warm loaves. "I may be dead, but I'm still hungry. I wonder if dead people are supposed to say blessings before they eat?"

Hayyim said the blessings — just to be sure. He sat on the cemetery wall, tearing off big chunks of bread and chewing them.

Other people came along on their way to and from market. Hayyim waved, but they all ran away, leaving behind the jam, sausage, cheese, and vegetables they were carrying.

"Being dead is not so bad," said Hayyim, helping himself to what they left in the road. "I have more to eat than when I was alive, and I don't have to do any work. I wish I could share some of this good food with my family. I suppose I'd better not try. The rabbi says that I have no place among the living. Still, I wish I had some company. This graveyard is a lonely place. I wonder where all the other dead people are?"

He was still wondering several days later, when he noticed something else. "These grave clothes are getting tight. Am I getting fat? This can't be! Dead people are supposed to wither away until nothing is left but bones. They're not supposed to gain weight. Something is wrong. I'd better visit the rabbi again."

Meanwhile, rumors about Hayyim's ghost had reached the rabbi. The rabbi set out for the cemetery to find out what was troubling the restless spirit. He hadn't gotten far when he saw Hayyim coming toward him.

The rabbi held up a holy book. "Spirit, come no closer!"

"That's fine with me, Rabbi," Hayyim answered. "We can talk from here. I need your advice. I have a problem. I don't think I'm dead."

The rabbi looked at him closely. "You look different, Hayyim. You've gained weight."

"I have. Dead people aren't supposed to do that. Are they?"

The rabbi came closer. He felt Hayyim's hands. He patted his belly. "Your flesh feels warm. I can touch you. You're alive!"

"That's what I thought," said Hayyim.

"How did you come to be wearing grave clothes? What made you think you were dead? And who did we bury in your grave?"

"I don't know. I only remember that Bayla Esther asked me to come to her inn to move chairs to the attic. . . ."

The rabbi listened. Finally, he said, "I think I understand what happened, especially since Bayla Esther's husband, Reb Aaron, hasn't been seen for several days. Hayyim, meet me at the inn after sundown. We need to have a word with Bayla Esther."

Bayla Esther grumbled to herself as
she sat at the kitchen table, counting her money by
the moonlight shining through the window. Her plan to bury
her husband had worked in a way she never expected. The rumor of
Hayyim's ghost had frightened people away from Horodenka. Since no
one came to town, no one stayed at the inn. Every room was empty.

Bayla Esther wondered what she was going to do, when she
heard a knock at the door.

"A guest at last!" She threw the door open. An eerie specter
stood on the threshold. It spoke in a quavering voice.

"Bayla Esther, it is I, Hayyim the porter! I have come back from
the grave to speak with you!"

"What nonsense!" Bayla Esther snapped. "You don't scare me,
Hayyim! You're no more a ghost than I am. I should know. Who do you
think took your clothes and wrapped
you in that shroud?"

"Why did you do that if I wasn't
dead?"

"So I could trick the Hevra Kadishah into burying my useless husband for free. Now I'll give you some advice. Get out of town and don't come back. You're ruining my business. If you don't disappear, I may have to find a way to get rid of you!"

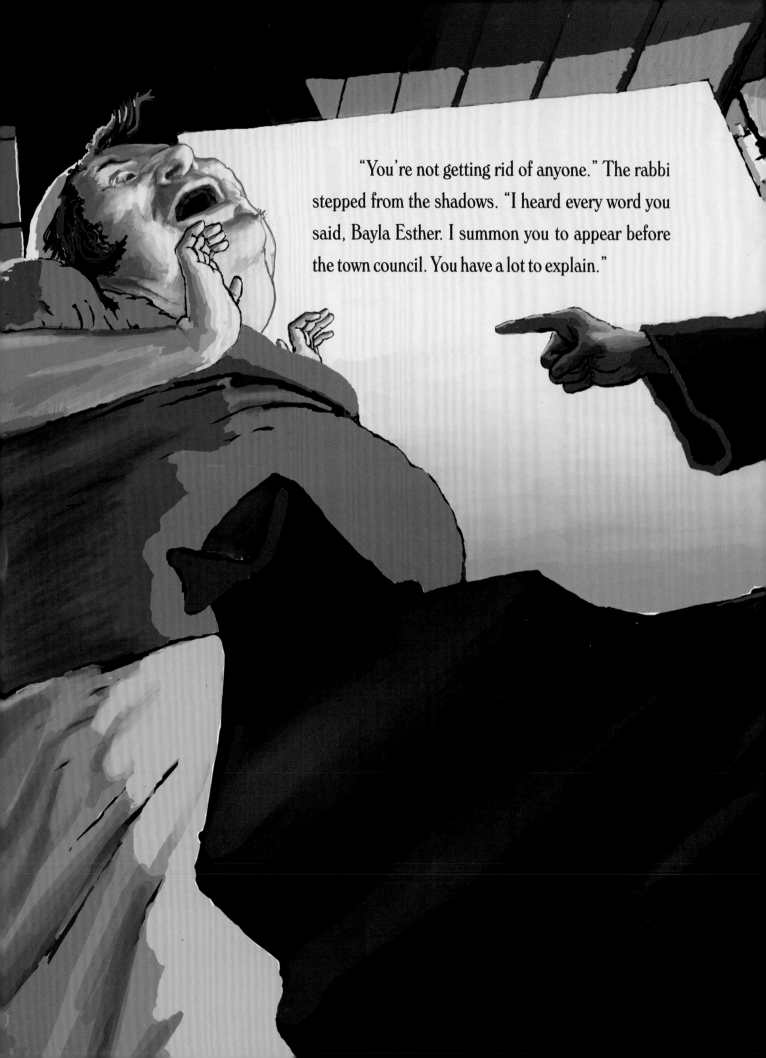

"You're not getting rid of anyone." The rabbi stepped from the shadows. "I heard every word you said, Bayla Esther. I summon you to appear before the town council. You have a lot to explain."

The Horodenka town council met the next day. The rabbi pronounced the judgement.

"Bayla Esther, you were too stingy to pay for one funeral, so you will now pay for two. Furthermore, you will compensate Hayyim's wife for the distress you caused. You will also give charity to the poor in your husband's name."

Bayla Esther had to agree. Within the year she sold the inn and moved away. It is said that Reb Aaron's ghost came back to haunt her. She troubled his days while he was alive, so he troubled her nights now that he was dead.

Hayyim the porter took over the inn. He and his family ran it for many years. When Hayyim died, he was buried in the Horodenka cemetery, where he rests to this day.

However, some people claim to have seen Hayyim's ghost sitting on the cemetery wall. He's a friendly ghost. He doesn't bother anybody and as far as anyone knows, he hasn't tried to return to the world of the living.